## Shan-Yu

Angered at the Great Wall of China, this fearsome enemy leader challenges the Emperor and the entire Imperial Army. He believes nothing will stand in his way.

## Shang

Recently promoted to Captain of the Imperial Recruits, Shang works hard to train his new soldiers. But he has a long way to go…

## Mushu

A tiny, self-important dragon that can talk his way through anything. But will he prove a real friend to Mulan and win back his place as an Ancestral Guardian?

# This Movie Magic belongs to:

..............................................

..............................................

All Ladybird books are available at most bookshops, supermarkets and newsagents, or can be ordered direct from:
**Ladybird Postal Sales** PO Box 133 Paignton TQ3 2YP England
*Telephone:* (+44) 01803 554761 *Fax:* (+44) 01803 663394

A catalogue record for this book is available from the British Library

Published by Ladybird Books Ltd
A subsidiary of the Penguin Group
A Pearson Company

LADYBIRD and the device of a Ladybird are trademarks of Ladybird Books Ltd Loughborough Leicestershire UK

© Disney MCMXCVIII

Adapted from Walt Disney Pictures' **Mulan**

Music by Matthew Wilder Lyrics by David Zippel Original score by Jerry Goldsmith
Produced by Pam Coats Directed by Barry Cook and Tony Bancroft

# DISNEY'S
# MULAN

Ladybird

Long ago, a wise emperor built a wall to protect China from invasion. It stretched for many miles and guarded the people like a great dragon.

But the fierce Hun leader, Shan-Yu, broke through the Great Wall, and led his warriors into China.

5

When the news reached the palace, the Emperor ordered his Chief Officer, Chi Fu, to call all the men of China to fight Shan-Yu.

"A single grain of rice can tip the scale. One man may be the difference between victory and defeat," he warned the Imperial Army Commander, General Li.

Far from the Imperial Palace, a teenage girl named Mulan was busily writing notes on her arm. Today was the day she was to be presented to the Matchmaker, and she wanted to be well prepared. A good match in marriage would bring honour to her family.

Suddenly Mulan realised she was late.

Mulan set to work quickly. She rewarded her dog, Little Brother, with a bone for helping her to feed the chickens. Then she prepared tea for her father, Fa Zhou.

Fa Zhou had once been a brave soldier, but he had been injured and now walked with a stick. Today he had just finished praying for his daughter in the Family Temple.

11

In the nearby village, Mulan's grandmother had just bought her granddaughter a cricket named Cri-Kee for good luck.

Mulan's mother, Fa Li, watched in horror as Grandmother Fa crossed the busy street. Carts and rickshaws swerved all around her.

"Yes! This cricket's a lucky one," proclaimed Grandmother Fa.

13

Mulan galloped into the village on her father's horse, Khan. She arrived in a cloud of dust. Her face was dirty and her untidy hair was full of grass stalks.

"I'm here!" she announced proudly, when she saw her mother.

With Fa Li's help, Mulan was soon transformed into a delicate Chinese maiden.

As a finishing touch, Fa Li gave Mulan a beautiful comb that had been in the family for many generations.

Then Grandmother Fa gave her an apple for serenity, a necklace for beauty, and Cri-Kee for good luck.

Unfortunately Mulan had little good luck when she met the Matchmaker. Everything went wrong.

Ink from Mulan's arm smeared over the Matchmaker's face. Cri-Kee went swimming in the tea, an incense-burner fell to the floor, and the Matchmaker's dress caught fire.

To put out the flames, Mulan quickly drenched the Matchmaker with tea. The Matchmaker was furious and ran outside.

"You may look like a bride," she screamed at Mulan, "but you will never bring your family honour."

Fa Li and Grandmother Fa led Mulan away.

Mulan could hardly hold her head up as she led Khan home. She had done the unthinkable and disgraced her family.

Staring at her image in the temple stones, Mulan knew that she could never be the delicate Chinese maiden that looked back at her.

Mulan sat tearfully under a tree in the garden. Her father quietly joined her and pointed up to a branch.

"This blossom's late," Fa Zhou said. "But I bet when it blooms, it will be the most beautiful."

Mulan smiled. She was forgiven.

But suddenly drums sounded in the distance and horses galloped into the village.

There was bad news. The Huns had invaded China, and one man from every family was ordered to serve in the Imperial Army.

To Mulan's horror, Fa Zhou stood forward for the Fa Family. She rushed to Chi Fu and begged him not to send her father to war. He was too lame to fight. But Chi Fu blamed Fa Zhou for his daughter's behaviour. Mulan had disgraced her family again.

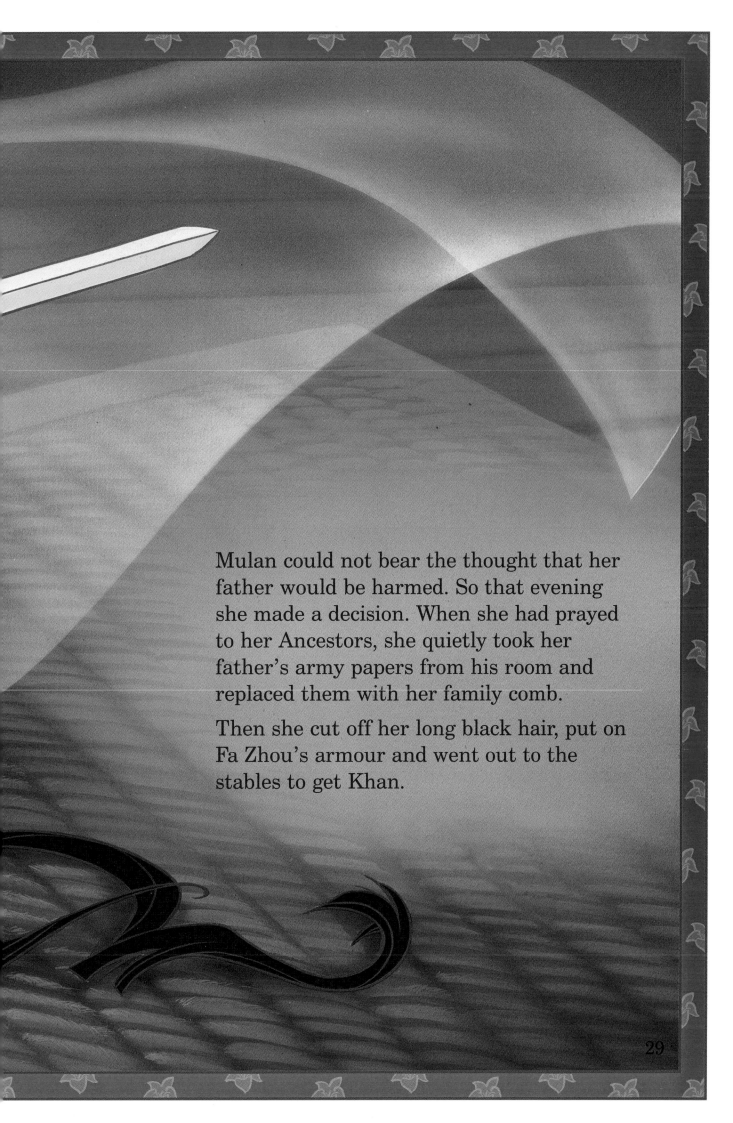

Mulan could not bear the thought that her father would be harmed. So that evening she made a decision. When she had prayed to her Ancestors, she quietly took her father's army papers from his room and replaced them with her family comb.

Then she cut off her long black hair, put on Fa Zhou's armour and went out to the stables to get Khan.

Mulan's only thought, as she headed out into the darkness, was to save her father's life.

A sudden crash of thunder woke the family. Something was wrong – Mulan was gone.

Fa Zhou saw the comb and rushed outside. But he was too late to stop her. She had taken his place in the Army. If someone found out she was a girl, she would be executed.

Meanwhile, the spirits of the Ancestors had gathered in the Fa Family Temple. They had decided to summon the most powerful of the Guardians to protect Mulan.

Mushu, a tiny, spirited dragon, thought they meant him. But the Ancestors just laughed. They couldn't leave this to Mushu. He'd made a big mistake before. Instead he was ordered to go outside to wake the Great Stone Dragon.

Mushu banged the statue on the head. But to his horror, it crumbled away to a heap of dust.

So Mushu disguised himself as the Great Stone Dragon. Then at Cri-Kee's suggestion, they went after Mulan.

Mushu was certain that if he made Mulan a hero, he would get his job as a Guardian back.

Next morning Mushu and Cri-Kee found Mulan outside the Army Camp. Mushu lit a fire and cast an impressive shadow against a rock. Then, in his mightiest voice, Mushu introduced himself as her Ancestral Guardian.

Mulan thought Mushu looked more like a lizard than a Guardian. But she needed all the help she could get.

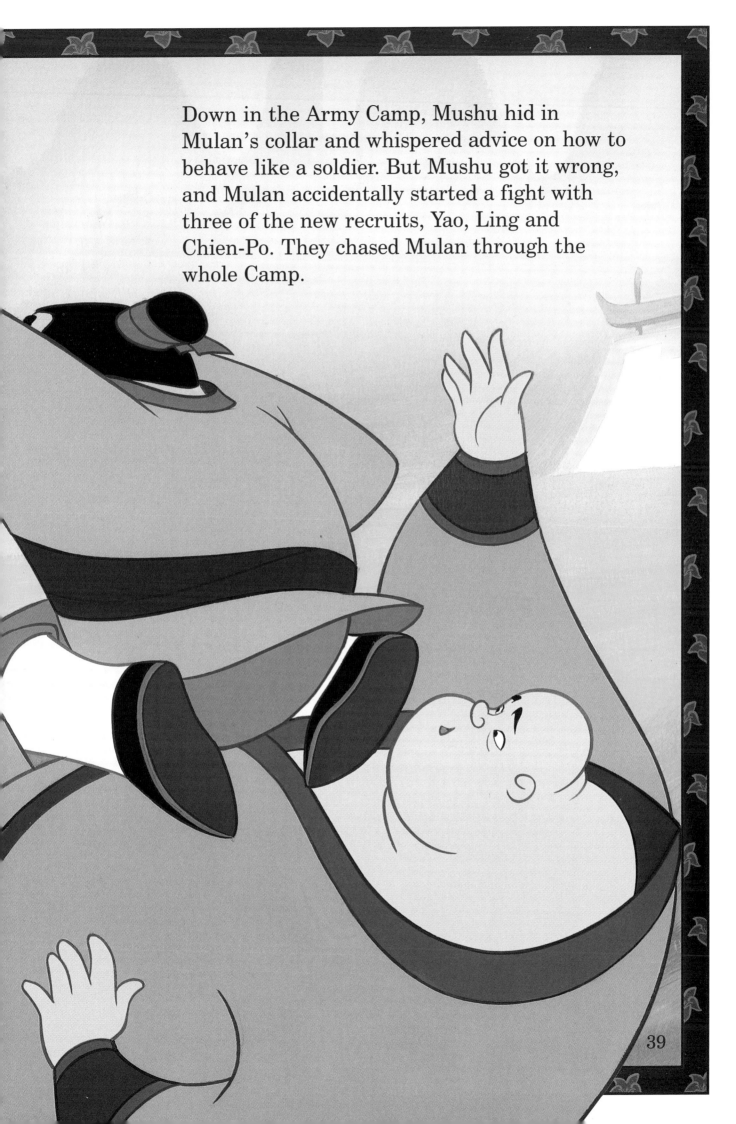

Down in the Army Camp, Mushu hid in Mulan's collar and whispered advice on how to behave like a soldier. But Mushu got it wrong, and Mulan accidentally started a fight with three of the new recruits, Yao, Ling and Chien-Po. They chased Mulan through the whole Camp.

39

Meanwhile, unaware of the scuffle outside, General Li was preparing to leave the Camp with the Main Army. He promoted his son, a young soldier called Shang, to be Captain over the new recruits while he was away. And he ordered Chi Fu to make a full report on Shang's progress.

Chi Fu was angry. He had wanted to be made Captain and he was jealous of Shang.

When the General had gone, Shang swiftly
brought the troops to order. He spoke sternly
to Mulan, "I don't need anyone causing
trouble in the Camp. Show me your papers."

Mulan handed them over. Shang was surprised
to learn that the Great Fa Zhou had a son. But
he accepted it and told the recruits to tidy up.

The next morning the recruits began their training. Their first exercise was to retrieve an arrow that Shang had shot to the top of a tall pole. To make it harder, they had to wear two large stone disks – one tied to each wrist.

"One disk represents discipline, the other strength," said Shang. "You need both to reach the arrow."

The recruits all tried in turn, but every one came crashing to the ground.

The tough training continued without a stop. Every day there was a new skill to learn and old skills to practise. But in each one, something seemed to go wrong.

Before long, Mulan was exhausted and eventually she collapsed. On the way back to Camp, Shang handed her Khan's reins. He ordered her to go home. Fa Zhou's son would never make a soldier.

As Mulan turned to look back at the Camp, she spotted the arrow embedded in the pole and realised at last how to achieve the task. She tied the weights together and pulled herself up.

The other recruits watched in amazement. Even Captain Shang had to admire her. She was accepted back into the Army.

Meanwhile, deep in the countryside, Shan-Yu's falcon had delivered a doll to his master. This gave Shan-Yu several clues about the Imperial Army. The doll had come from the Tung-Shao Pass, where General Li's Army would be waiting.

"Come," Shan-Yu told his men with a sinister sneer. "The little girl must be missing her doll. We should return it to her."

That night Mulan crept to the lake to bathe. But soon Ling, Yao and Chien-Po came along and jumped into the water. Mulan tried to swim to the side, and Mushu came to her rescue. He dived into the water, headed for Ling and bit him. The soldiers swam to the side, fearing there was a snake.

"Uggh, what a nasty flavour!" groaned Mushu. But at least Mulan had got away.

Mushu knew that in order to impress the Fa Family Ancestors, he would have to get Mulan into battle. So when Mulan had returned to her tent, Mushu got Cri-Kee to help him to write a letter from General Li. It ordered Shang and his men to meet him at the Tung-Shao Pass.

They passed the urgent message to Chi Fu, who ran to tell the Captain.

As Shang and his troops headed into the mountains, they entered a village that had been burned out by the Huns. Signs of battle lay all around, and Chien-Po found General Li's helmet in the rubble. The entire Imperial Army had been destroyed.

Shang silently honoured his father. Mulan placed a doll she had found on the battlefield next to the helmet. She didn't know it was the clue that had led Shan-Yu to the Army's position.

"We're the only hope for the Emperor now," Shang said to his soldiers. "Move out!"

Shang and his men marched out into the Pass. But Mushu accidentally shot a rocket from the munitions wagon and gave away their position to the enemy. Instantly thousands of flaming Hun arrows showered down from the mountains.

Mulan cut Khan loose from the wagon, just before it exploded. Mushu and Cri-Kee were thrown to safety.

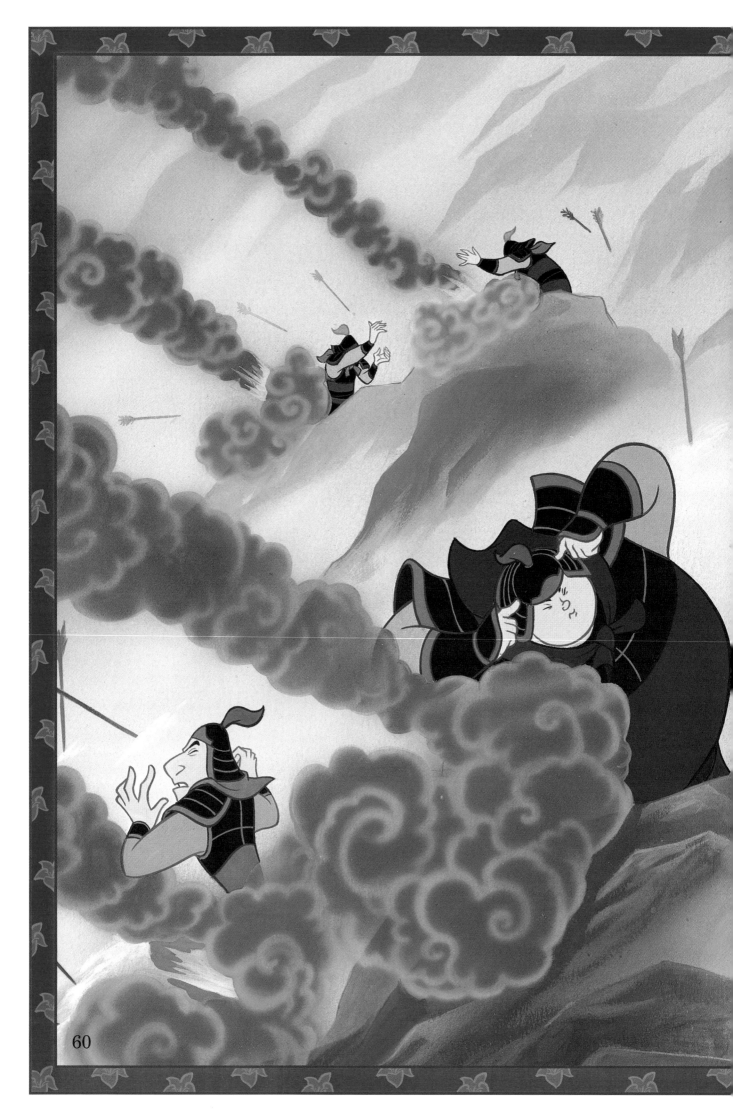

Hundreds of Hun warriors came over the mountain top. Hopelessly outnumbered, Shang ordered Yao to point the last cannon at Shan-Yu.

But Mulan had another idea. She grabbed the cannon and ran towards the Huns. Then she forced Mushu to light the fuse.

The rocket flew through the air and landed in the mountain, causing a massive avalanche. The Huns were buried in the snow.

Shan-Yu was furious and wanted revenge on the soldier who had destroyed his warriors. He struck Mulan with his sword and tried to ride away. But soon he too was buried in the snow.

Yao, Ling and Chien-Po took shelter with the other soldiers under some rocks, but Mulan and Captain Shang were still in grave danger.

Khan raced to Mulan's rescue, and she reached out her hand to save Shang. But a wall of snow threw them apart.

Some time later Mulan found Shang lying unconscious in the snow. She lifted him onto Khan.

When the snow had settled, the
other soldiers used an arrow and a
rope to pull Mulan and her friends
up to safety.

Shang regained consciousness and
Mulan was proclaimed the Hero.
But soon she collapsed in pain.
Mulan awoke in the doctor's tent
to find that her secret had been
discovered. They had found out she
was a girl, and it was the Captain's
duty to execute her.

"A life for a life," said Shang, refusing to kill her. Then he ordered the troops to go home.

Mulan was left in the mountains with Mushu, Cri-Kee and Khan. They watched in horror, as Shan-Yu and five Hun warriors emerged from the snow and headed for the Imperial City.

Mulan caught up with Shang just as he and his troops were approaching the Imperial Palace. She tried to warn him that the Emperor was in danger.

But Shang refused to believe her again.

Shang walked up the steps of the Imperial Palace and bowed to present Shan-Yu's sword to the Emperor.

Suddenly Shan-Yu's falcon swooped down, grabbed the sword and delivered it to Shan-Yu. He had been waiting in hiding.

Then five Hun warriors slashed their way out of a paper dragon and imprisoned the Emperor in a palace tower.

Nearby Mulan had devised a plan. Quickly she helped Ling, Yao and Chien-Po to disguise themselves as girls. Then she led them to the side of the palace, where they wrapped their dress sashes round a pillar. Skilfully, they began to climb.

Shang came to join them.

Once inside the Imperial Palace, Mulan and her friends knocked out the Hun warriors who were guarding the tower. Meanwhile Shang rushed onto the balcony, where the Emperor was being held, and confronted Shan-Yu.

Chien-Po ran to the Emperor and carried him to the edge where they slid down a makeshift line. Ling and Yao followed. Quickly, Mulan cut the line and turned to face Shan-Yu.

Furious that the Emperor had escaped, Shan-Yu put his sword to Shang's neck. "You took away my victory," he snarled.

"No!" said Mulan. "I did!" Then she pulled back her hair so Shan-Yu would recognise her.

"The soldier from the mountains," roared Shan-Yu. He let Shang go and chased Mulan out onto the rooftop.

Everything was going according to plan.
Mulan grabbed his sword and pinned down
his cloak.

Mushu floated over with a rocket strapped to
his back, and Cri-Kee lit the fuse. As Mushu
jumped to safety, the rocket swept Shan-Yu all
the way to the munitions tower.

Shan-Yu was destroyed. But the force of the
explosion catapulted Mushu and Cri-Kee
safely through the air, and Mulan was thrown
on top of Shang.

An entire wing of the Imperial Palace burst
into flames and fireworks lit up the City.

The Emperor and Chi Fu approached.

"I've heard a great deal about you, Fa Mulan," the Emperor said, sternly. "You stole your father's armour, impersonated a soldier, dishonoured the Chinese Army, destroyed my palace, and... saved us all."

Then the Emperor did something amazing. He bowed to Mulan... and everyone followed his example.

The Emperor presented Mulan with his
medallion and Shan-Yu's sword to honour her
family. Then Shang said an awkward goodbye.

"The flower that blooms in adversity is the
most rare and beautiful of all," the Emperor
said to Shang.

The next day Mulan presented the Emperor's gifts to her father. "The greatest honour is having you for a daughter," said Fa Zhou.

At that moment, Shang came into the garden. To the delight of the entire family, Mulan invited him to dinner.

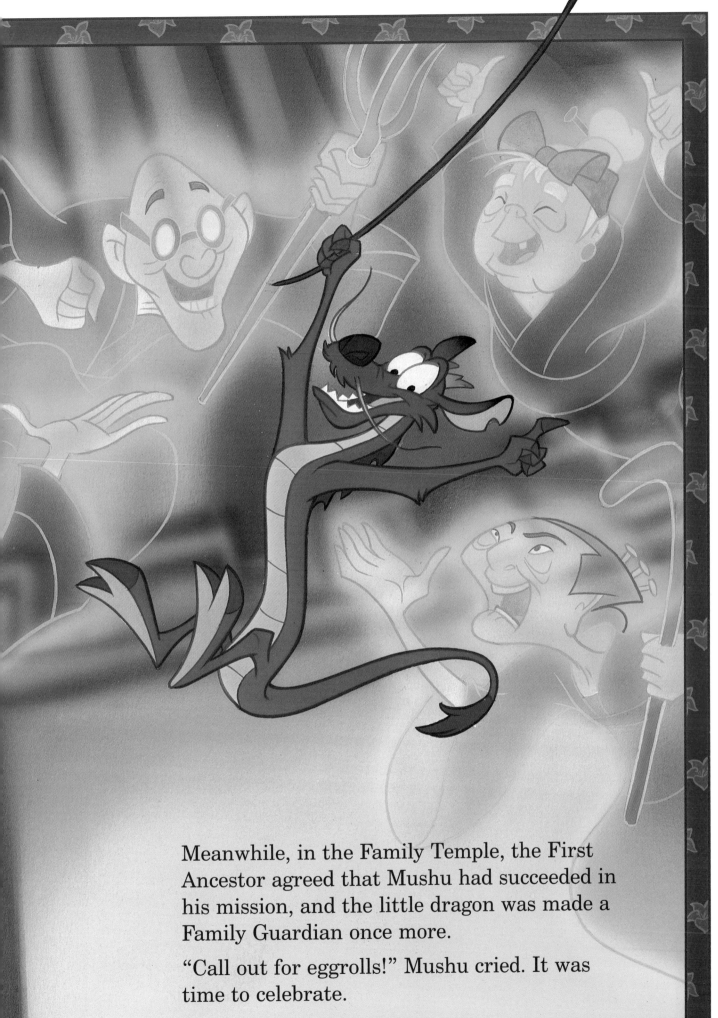

Meanwhile, in the Family Temple, the First
Ancestor agreed that Mushu had succeeded in
his mission, and the little dragon was made a
Family Guardian once more.

"Call out for eggrolls!" Mushu cried. It was
time to celebrate.

# Mulan

When Mulan is shamed by the Matchmaker, there seems little hope that she can bring honour to her family. But her courage and high spirits win out.

# Fa Zhou

A once-famous Chinese soldier, Mulan's father does not expect to have to fight again. But, when Shan-Yu invades, Fa Zhou prepares for war, despite his wounds.

# Cri-Kee

Yes, this cricket is a lucky one (sometimes!) and he is Mulan's companion through thick and thin. Can he help her to bring honour to her family?